PUFFIN BOOKS

The Boomerang Book

Do you know how to make a boomerang bounce ? Can you throw it so that it circles a tree or post and then returns to you ? Can you make it fly back past you and then return to you ?

In this book M. J. Hanson tells you how to make and throw your own boomerangs. He gives clear step-by-step instructions for both right-handed and left-handed boomerang throwers and with a little patience and a little woodwork skill you will produce a boomerang that will make you the envy of your friends.

Join the ancient art of boomerang throwing. It's fun, it's cheap and it's catching.

Illustrated with line drawings and photographs

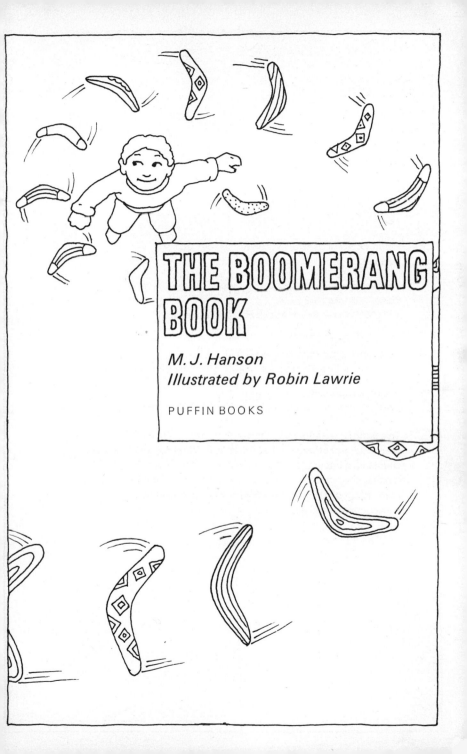

THE BOOMERANG BOOK

M. J. Hanson
Illustrated by Robin Lawrie

PUFFIN BOOKS

Puffin Books: a Division of Penguin Books Ltd,
Harmondsworth,.Middlesex, England

Penguin Books Australia Ltd, Ringwood, Victoria, Australia
Penguin Books (N.Z.) Ltd,
182–190 Wairau Road, Auckland 10, New Zealand

First published 1974
Text copyright © M. J. Hanson, 1974
Illustrations Copyright © 1974 by Robin Lawrie

Made and printed in Great Britain by
Lowe & Brydone (Printers) Ltd, Thetford, Norfolk

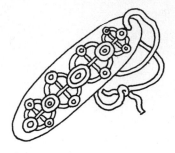

To my wife and children

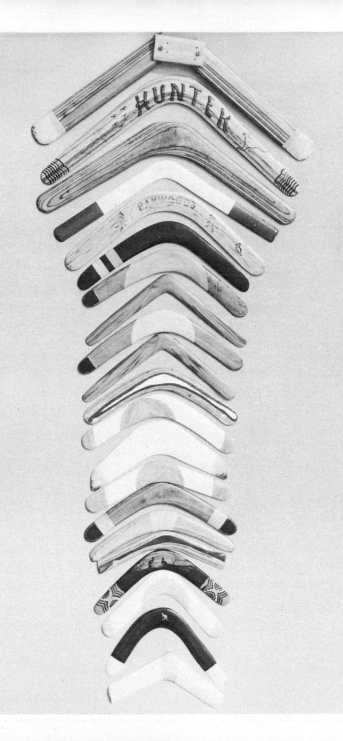

Fig. 1

Introduction

My purpose in writing this book is to introduce you to boomerangs and, more particularly, to explain how to make and throw the returning type used by Australian Aborigines.

The construction is quite straightforward for anyone with a little woodworking skill, and the knack of throwing a boomerang so it returns is easily learned with some practice.

In the future I hope there will be hundreds of boomerangs spinning their intricate paths through the sky.

1 About Boomerangs

The boomerang is one of the oldest weapons used by man. It was in use many centuries ago, long before bows and arrows were invented. (One boomerang has been discovered that is 2,400 years old, according to the archaeologists who found it.)

The first explorer to meet the Australian Aborigines and see boomerangs was Captain James Cook when he landed at Botany Bay in

1770. In his ship's log he described his meetings with the Aborigines and the weapons they used: darts with shark's teeth fixed in them and spear slings capable of launching a spear, that were 'as accurate as a musket at fifty yards'.

Indeed the Aborigines used (and still do use) a variety of weapons made with great skill and patience from simple materials. The spear sling described by Captain Cook was called a 'woomera' and was used to launch spears eight or nine feet long (2.4–2.7m). The point of the spear was dipped in the poisonous sap of the mangrove tree, so if it caused a wound it was almost sure to be infected. You may also have heard of the 'bull-roarer', a piece of wood tied to a string that makes a fearful noise, a bit like a football rattle, when you spin it around your head. The 'bull-roarer' was used to scare animals.

Apart from these intriguing weapons, the Australian Aborigines are better known for their remarkable boomerangs (Fig. 1). 'Boomerang' is

a very odd word. It is a native word of the Turuwal tribe of Aborigines, who lived near the Georges River in New South Wales, and may have come from the Aboriginal word 'boomori', wind.

The Aborigines used three types of boomerang:

1. The Ritual Boomerang Some tribal ceremonies were performed with the aid of these ritual boomerangs, but very little is known about them.

2. The Non-Returning Boomerang This could be a lethal weapon in an expert's hands. It was capable of killing a bird or knocking out a 'boomer' (a large kangaroo) if it scored a direct hit. Careful shaping enabled it to be thrown much further than an ordinary piece of wood.

3. The Returning Boomerang This was (and still is) used mainly for sport and games. Tournaments were held in which the competitors vied with each other to see who could make their boomerang fly the most intricate path or land nearest to a marker on the ground. The returning boomerang was not really a weapon but was used to train men in dodging weapons and to frighten flocks of ducks, cockatoos or parakeets when it was thrown above them. The birds were alarmed by the odd noise it made, which sounds not unlike the cry of a hawk, and flew lower, only to be trapped in the nets the Aborigines spread between trees (Fig. 2).

In this book we are mainly concerned with returning boomerangs. Boomerangs are made of

Fig. 2

mulga or mangrove wood. The wood of the mangrove tree is very hard and the Aborigines also made shields from its bark. The Aborigines used rough implements to shape the wood, and the vital twist that makes the boomerang return was made by first heating it in hot ashes and then soaking it in water. Most boomerangs were highly decorated with dyes extracted from plants.

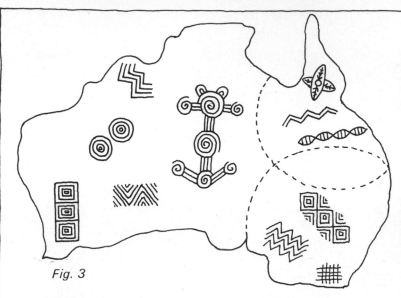

Fig. 3

Aborigines in different parts of Australia used different decorations on their boomerangs. The map (Fig. 3) shows what decorations were common where; and you can see some decorated boomerangs in the drawing (Fig. 4).

Most people think that the Australian Aborigines were the only people to use boomerangs, but this is not so. 'Throwing sticks' were used by the Ancient Egyptians for killing birds; by the Hopi Indian tribe, in what is now Arizona and California; by the people of Southern India; and by Africans, Eskimos and Polynesians. They are still used by some tribes in North East Africa and in India where, today, they are made of ivory or steel.

But it is the Australian Aborigines who discovered how to make returning boomerangs. All the other boomerangs are the non-returning type.

Returning boomerangs are anything from twelve to thirty inches (300–762mm) in length and the shape varies from a gentle curve to a sharp angle. The top surface of the boomerang is curved, while the bottom is flat. These are the

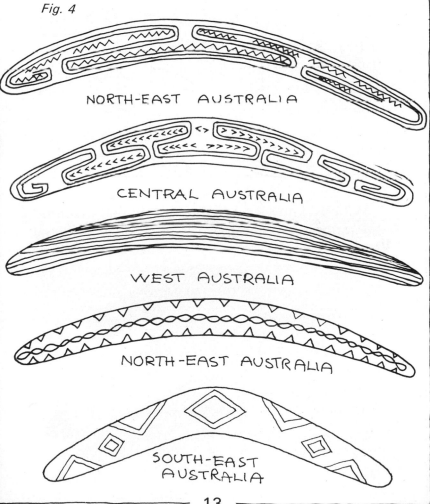

Fig. 4

NORTH-EAST AUSTRALIA

CENTRAL AUSTRALIA

WEST AUSTRALIA

NORTH-EAST AUSTRALIA

SOUTH-EAST AUSTRALIA

shapes of the different boomerangs (Fig. 5).
(Imagine what a nasty injury could be caused by
the hook on boomerang C!) These are some
of *my* returning boomerangs (Fig. 6).

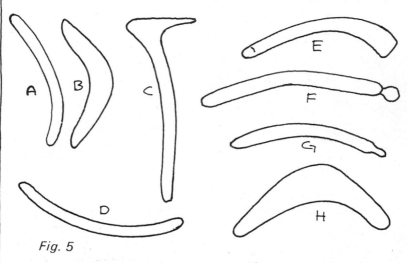

Fig. 5

Nobody knows how the Aborigines invented
the returning boomerang, but it was probably

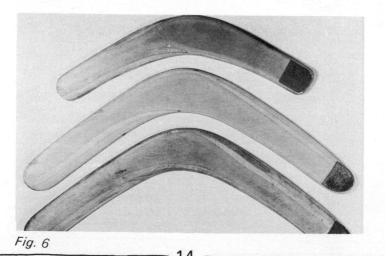

Fig. 6

developed from a non-returning type that curved in flight because it was unintentionally twisted.

Many people who have never seen a boomerang thrown think it flies away and returns along the same straight line; but if you look at Fig. 7 you will see how wrong they are. Those intricate curves are the flight paths of boomerangs viewed from different directions.

In the space of a minute or two, you can make a small cardboard boomerang for use indoors.

Fig. 7

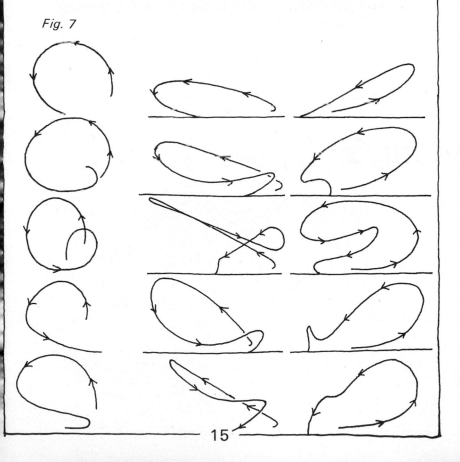

Important note:

The instructions given in this book are for both right- and left-handed boomerangs. Those of you who are left-handed will want a left-handed boomerang and those who are right-handed will need a right-handed one. So, in some of the illustrations two diagrams are given. One is labelled R.H. (right-handed) and the other labelled L.H. (left-handed).

The single illustrations are right-handed. You can easily convert a right-handed illustration into a left-handed one by holding a mirror and looking at the image (Fig. 8).

Fig. 8

2 A Cardboard Boomerang

All you need to make your Mark I boomerang is a piece of stiff card and a pair of scissors.

First cut the card into the shape shown in Fig. 9. You can make it anything from three to six inches (76–152mm) long. Bend up the front of the tip

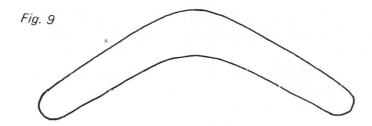

Fig. 9

of the card just a little along the line AC (Fig. 10). Getting this bend right is rather important.

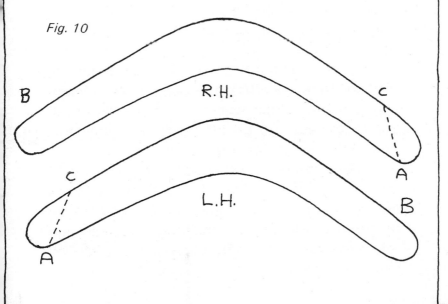

Fig. 10

Looking from the front you should see something like Fig. 11.

Fig. 11

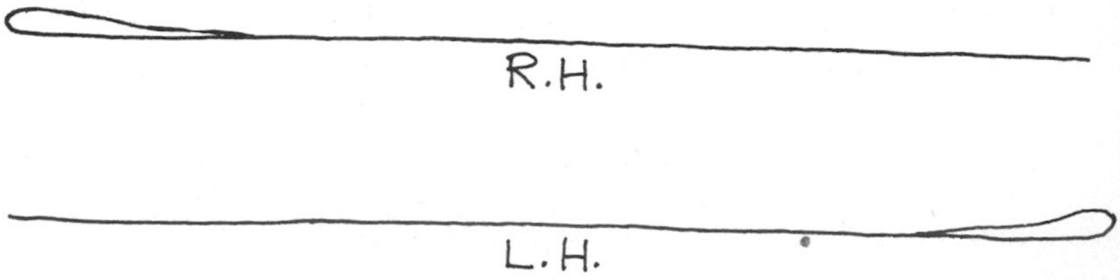

R.H.

L.H.

Now gently grip your boomerang on a support (this book will do) with your thumb in the middle so that the slight twist AC is turning up a little towards you (Fig. 12). Now give the edge of arm B a good flick with your finger so it spins away from under your thumb. If the first flight isn't very impressive don't despair; try again. If your boomerang quickly stops spinning and falls to the floor, check that you only gave the tip a small twist.

Soon you should grasp the technique of flicking. Now try tilting the support at different angles to see which suits your boomerang best. Each boomerang flies differently and you must find the best angle for your own boomerang.

Now try making another boomerang, or twisting the tip a little more or a little less, and you will see that the flight is different. If you twist the tip up more it should turn in a tighter circle and return in a shorter time. If you twist it less, its orbit should be greater.

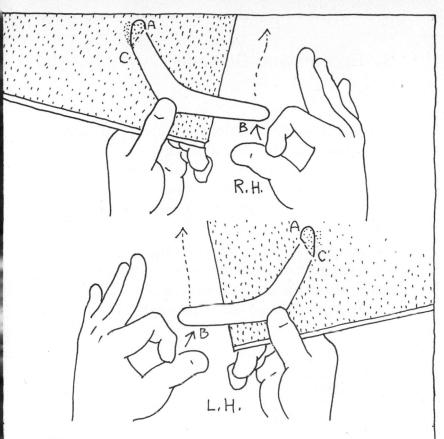

Fig. 12

By holding the support at different angles you may be able to make your boomerang follow some of the flight paths in Fig. 7.

Before progressing to the real thing – a wooden version of the Mark I boomerang – it is important to look at some of the scientific principles involved in its flight.

3 Boomerang Science

The Australian Aborigines were experts in boomerang construction and throwing as a result of centuries of experience, but they did not understand why a boomerang returned when they threw it. The secret of boomerang flight still confounds many people.

No two boomerangs will perform in an identical way. The surfaces of their arms cannot be exactly identical and so, as the boomerang spins through the air, the effect of the wind on the surfaces is slightly different on each one. Sometimes, but not always, the lifting arm is slightly lighter than the other and has an angled tip. The other arm is often called the 'dingle' arm (Fig. 13).

Fig. 13

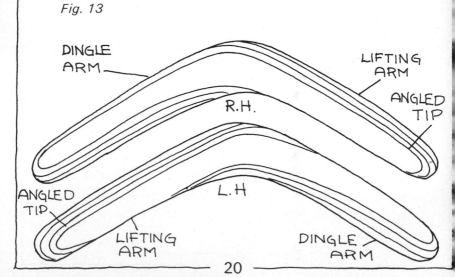

The first person to understand fully why a boomerang returns to the thrower was the scientist T. L. Mitchell, who wrote an article about boomerangs in 1842. A fully detailed explanation of boomerang flight is very complicated, so I will just deal with the most important points here.

The flight of a boomerang is governed by two well-known scientific principles:

1. The force of lift on a curved surface caused by air flowing over it (as with an aeroplane's wing).

2. The unwillingness of a spinning gyroscope to move from its position. (A gyroscope is a heavy wheel spinning in a frame.) Once a gyroscope is set spinning it is difficult to alter its position (Fig. 14).

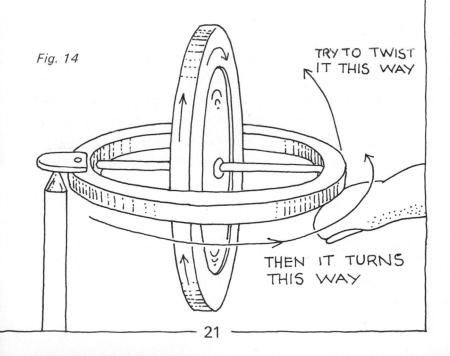

Fig. 14

TRY TO TWIST IT THIS WAY

THEN IT TURNS THIS WAY

Let us look closely at these in turn.

1. You can demonstrate this first principle for yourself if you cut a piece of card and bend it to

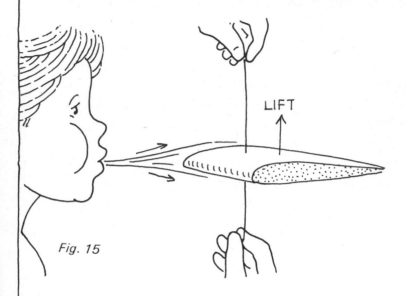

LIFT

Fig. 15

the shape shown in Fig. 15. Fix it with tape and with a needle thread a length of cotton through the centre line about one third of the way back from the blunt edge. Hold the cotton vertically and blow hard at the blunt edge. Your 'wing' should ride up the cotton. We say the surface generates LIFT. An aeroplane's wing looks like this, and so do the rotor blades of a helicopter. The wings, or arms of a boomerang have surfaces roughly the same shape as your 'wing'.

2. If you have ever had a gyroscope you will know that if you try to twist it while it is spinning an odd

thing happens. It does not turn as you wish it to but tries to turn in a different direction. We say it PRECESSES. If you have never played with a gyroscope, Fig. 14 will explain what I mean. A fast-spinning bicycle wheel makes a good gyroscope. Perhaps you could experiment with one. A spinning boomerang is like a gyroscope. From a bird's-eye view it precesses and curves in circles (Fig. 7).

But how do these two scientific principles cause a boomerang to return?

Well, firstly, a boomerang acts like a heli-copter's rotor as it spins. A helicopter's rotor and a spinning boomerang are shown in Fig. 16. You

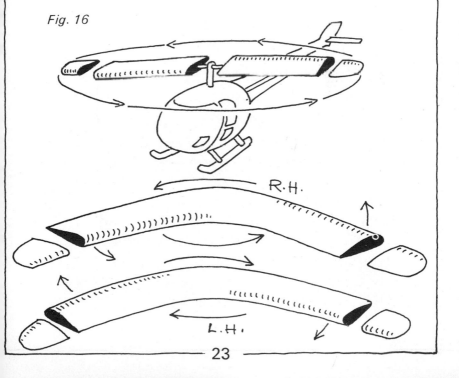

Fig. 16

can see that the two are very much alike. The rotor lifts the helicopter and the boomerang lifts itself. As the boomerang is released by an expert thrower he causes it to spin vertically (see the photographs on pages –). The vertically spinning boomerang will still generate lift but the lift force will not be upwards; it will be to one side (Fig. 17).

Fig. 17

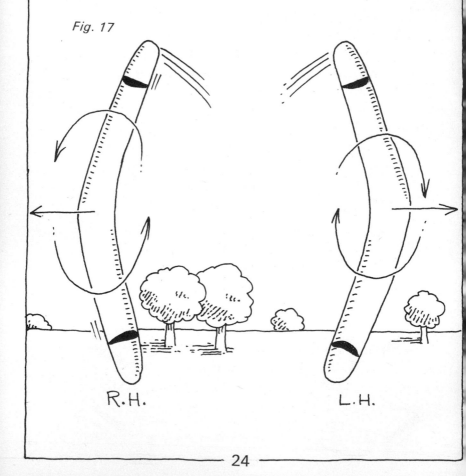

R.H.

L.H.

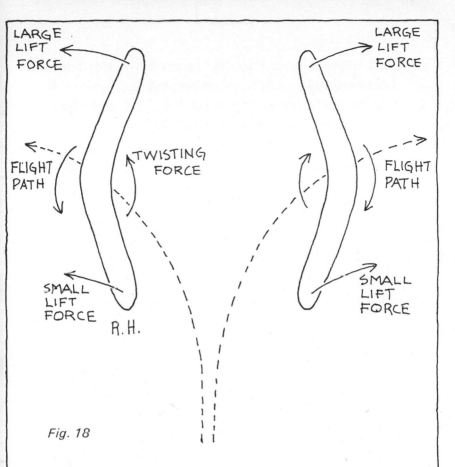

LARGE LIFT FORCE

LARGE LIFT FORCE

FLIGHT PATH

TWISTING FORCE

FLIGHT PATH

SMALL LIFT FORCE

R.H.

SMALL LIFT FORCE

Fig. 18

Now, as the boomerang spins vertically and moves forward, air flows faster over the top arm, at a certain instant, than over the bottom arm. The top arm therefore generates more lift than the bottom arm and the boomerang tries to twist itself; but, as it is spinning fast, it acts like a gyroscope and precesses or turns to the side in an arc (Fig. 18). If it flies for long enough it will turn a full circle and return to the thrower. The tip of the boomerang is angled to give it a smaller orbit and make it easier to throw properly, but some boomerangs do not have an angled tip.

A typical boomerang orbit (Fig. 19) may have a diameter of 60–90 feet (18–27m) and a height

Fig. 19

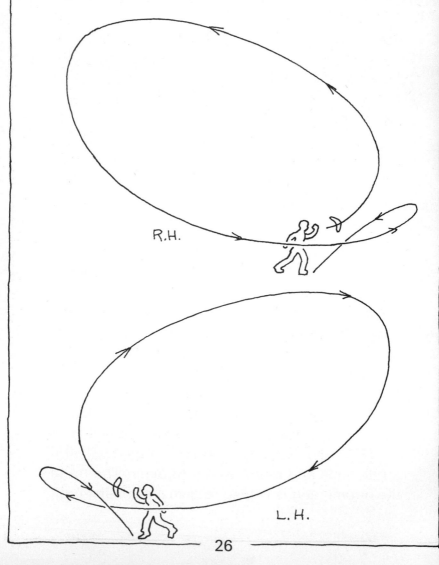

of about 30 feet (9m), or, as high as a double-decker bus is long. Every boomerang has a 'built-in' orbit diameter. This means you cannot make one boomerang spin orbits of different diameters. Throwing it harder or spinning it faster makes no difference, its orbit will remain the same.

When a boomerang is properly launched it will spin vertically at first and then 'lie down' or spin horizontally for the rest of its flight. It will spin round about ten times each second and move forward at about sixty miles (94km) per hour. That is five or six times faster than your fastest sprint or as fast as a cricket ball can be thrown. A typical flight lasts up to ten seconds. Scientists have used a computer to calculate an ideal boomerang orbit, and the path predicted by the computer is almost exactly the same as a boomerang's actual path.

4   A Wooden Boomerang

You can make a boomerang in just a few hours with modern tools, whereas the Australian Aborigine took days to shape patiently the hard wood with his primitive tools.

All you need for shaping a boomerang is a *coping* or *fret saw,* a *rasp* or *spokeshave* and *sandpaper.* If you have some wood-working ability you should be able to manage quite well, but if you are not sure you can cope, then you had best ask for help or advice.

Make your boomerang from plywood, which is even better than mangrove or mulga wood as it is not so liable to split along the grain. You need a piece of $\frac{1}{4}''$ or $\frac{5}{16}''$ (6 mm or 8 mm) good-quality plywood measuring about 16" × 6" (40·6 cm × 15·24 cm). Copy out the shape onto graph paper (Fig. 20) and then onto the wood. The squares are 1" × 1" (25·4mm. × 25·4mm.).

Fig. 20

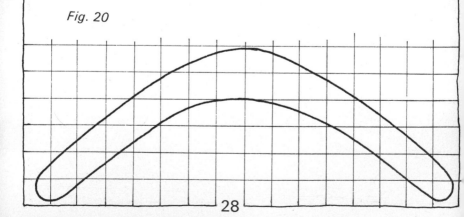

Reproduce the shape as best you can. With a coping saw or fret saw carefully cut out the shape.

The next stage requires a little patience and care as you now have to shape the surfaces. The

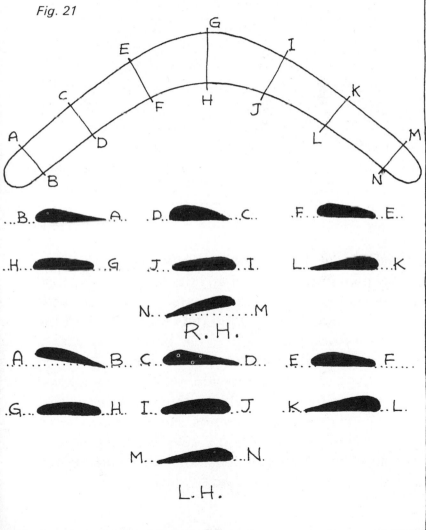

Fig. 21

R.H.

L.H.

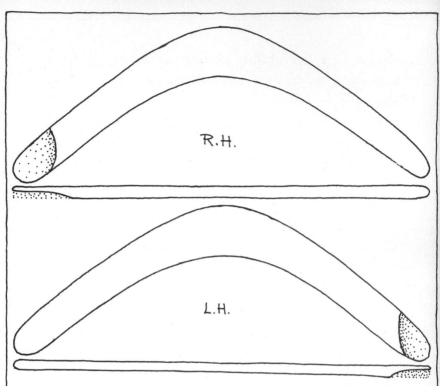

Fig. 22

shapes at different points on the boomerang are shown in Fig. 21. Half an hour's work with a rasp or spokeshave and you should have the surfaces about right. If the going gets tough think of the poor Aborigine shaping his boomerang with a sharp stone under the hot desert sun.

Start with the underside, which is completely flat save for the tip, which is shaved away so that it inclines slightly upwards. Fig. 22 shows what this tip looks like when viewed from the bottom and front. (Do you remember that you twisted the tip on your cardboard boomerang?)

Now you must shape the top surfaces. This needs a little care. Look carefully at Fig. 21. The shapes BA, DC, FE etc. are the shapes you would see if you cut through the boomerang along the lines. You will notice that one tip is inclined slightly upwards: this is the tip that you first shaved away. The edges BDF and IKM are blunt edges on the right-handed boomerang but the sharp edges on the left-handed boomerang. In the middle (GH) you must merge the surfaces smoothly. Fig. 23 shows you the surfaces.

Don't worry too much about exactly matching the shapes in the drawings because as long as they are reasonably correct the boomerang will still work. Do remember, though, that the better the shaping, the better the boomerang will fly. The shapes of the surfaces on one of my boomerangs can be seen in Figs. 24 and 25.

Fig. 23

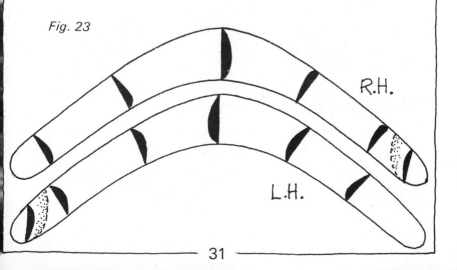

R.H.

L.H.

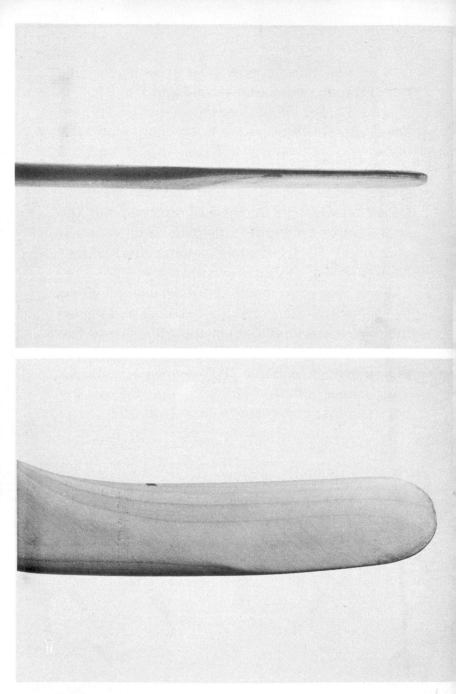

Fig. 24

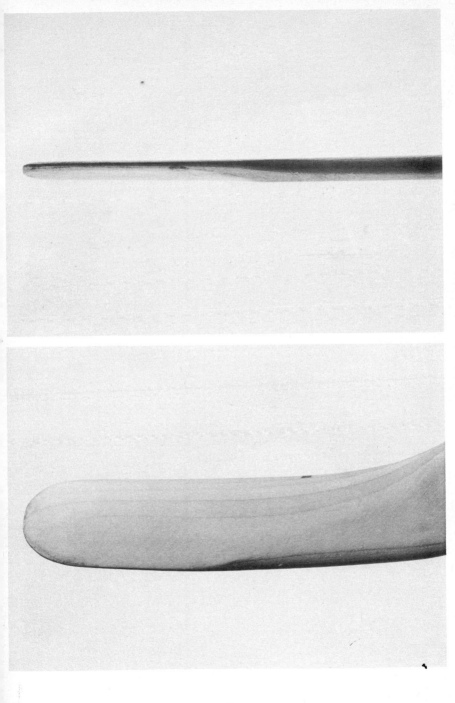

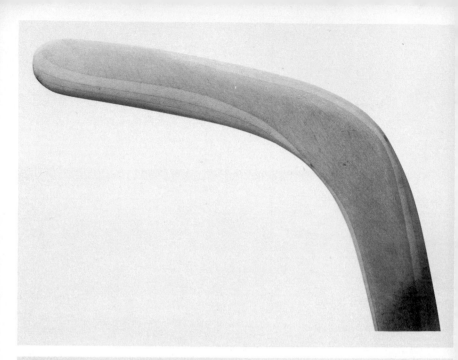

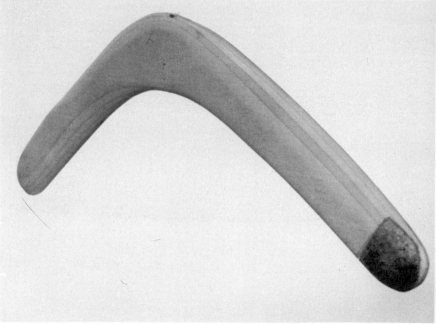

Fig. 25

34

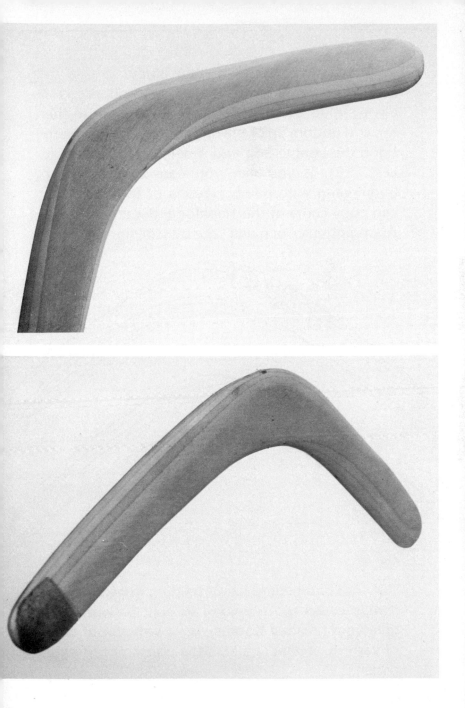

Now you must use a little elbow grease to sandpaper smooth all the surfaces and edges. I always glue a piece of coarse sandpaper to the top and bottom tip of the dingle arm. This is where I grip the boomerang and it helps me to throw it (Fig. 26): If you like you can decorate your boomerang with paint, crayons or felt-tips. You can copy some of the traditional decorations the Aborigines use, or make your own designs.

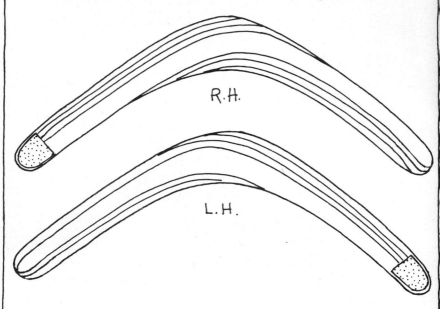

R.H.

L.H.

Fig. 26

If your boomerang keeps landing in damp grass it may cause the plywood to split or warp, so, give your finished boomerang a waterproof coat of varnish, shellac, paint, shoe polish or furniture polish.

5   The Art of Throwing

In acquiring any skill, be it mountaineering, acting, painting or boomerang throwing, patience and practice make perfect. Boomerang throwing is not a dangerous sport but it can be if you are not careful. Plywood is strong, but it can split if it is involved in an argument with a tree, wall or any solid object. Also, don't forget that although the human body is strong too, it can be hurt if it is hit by a returning boomerang!

So, find an open field free of obstructions or bystanders. How is the wind? If you can feel a breeze on your face go home and bring out your kite. Every day is not a boomerang day.

When you are alone in the middle of a field on a calm day, grip your boomerang by the dingle arm as shown in Fig. 27. (Aborigines grasp the lifting arm. It is a matter of choice but if you have glued sand-paper to the tip as I suggested, then grip it my way.) Now, try and throw it.

You will probably find it falls to the ground in an ungainly fashion. (Lucky there were no by-standers!) You may have to jump out of the way to avoid your returning boomerang the first time you throw it.

Here are the three secrets to success:
1. If there is a very light wind, find out its direction by dropping a few blades of grass, then throw

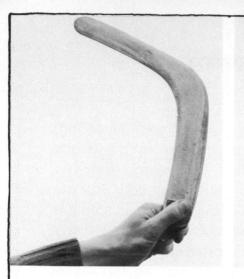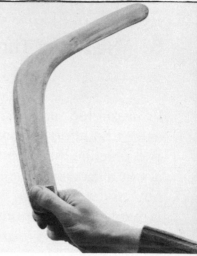

Fig. 27

your boomerang to one side of where the breeze is coming from (Fig. 28).

2. Spin the boomerang rather than throw it. Flick it really hard as you bring your arm forward and let it pull itself from your grasp by its own impetus.

3. Don't spin it horizontally. Make it spin almost vertically when you launch it and aim it slightly upwards. Figs. 29 and 30 should give you a good idea.

If you bear these points in mind your boomerang should partially return to you after a few attempts.

If your boomerang almost returns but falls to the ground some way in front of you, then spin it harder, throw it up more, or launch it so it is spinning not quite vertically but slightly tilted. If it returns too well and falls to the ground behind you, then spin it less or don't throw it up so much.

A boomerang thrown so that it spins horizontally will return, but it will not travel in an orbit, it will just rise and fall.

An hour's practice should make you quite competent. You will learn how important it is to judge the right amount of spin, the direction of throw, and the angle at which the boomerang is spinning. During your practice you should have made your boomerang perform some of the flight

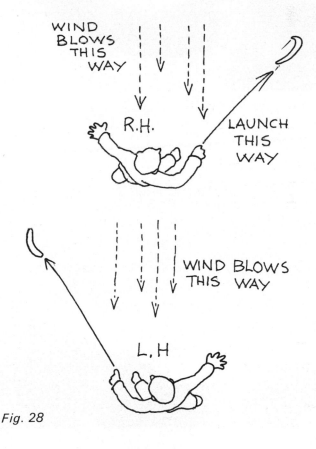

WIND
BLOWS
THIS
WAY

R.H.

LAUNCH
THIS
WAY

WIND BLOWS
THIS WAY

L.H

Fig. 28

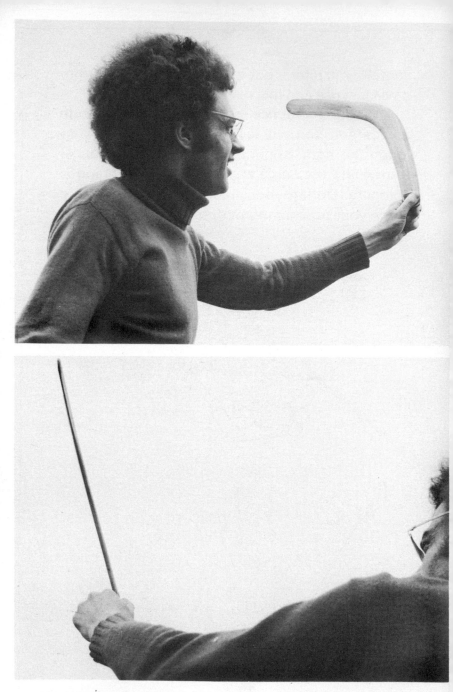

Fig. 29

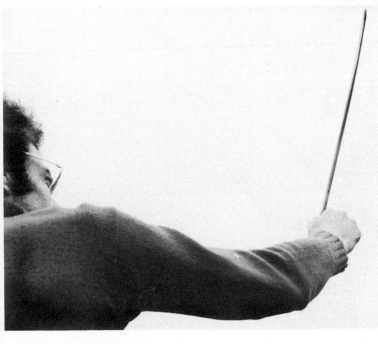

Fig. 30

paths shown earlier in the book. Your wrist will probably ache, so go home and rest it.

The next time you practice, try and make your boomerang hover near you before falling to the ground. This trick will make you the envy of all your friends. You will be able to catch it on the return. When it is hovering near you, try clapping your hands to make a boomerang sandwich. It is best to catch it at the middle as this part is not spinning so fast as the tips. Wear a pair of thick gloves when you practise catching the boomerang, and please remember that if a spinning boomerang strikes you in the face, a visit to the hospital or dentist will probably result.

Have fun then, but be aware of the hazards. Be careful!

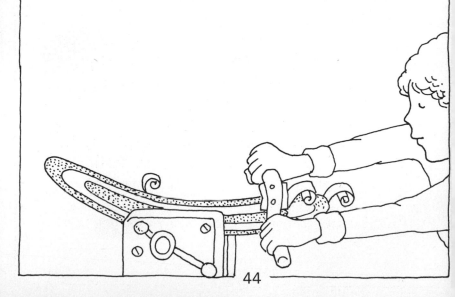

6 The Experts

It will take months if not years of practice to become as good as the Australian Aborigines, who can throw a boomerang and make it return with remarkable accuracy. I have heard of (but never seen) throwers who can hold out their palm and their returning boomerang hovers and falls gently into it.

The furthest a boomerang has ever been thrown is 250 yards (230m) in a circular path. This is much further than the best cricket ball throw at 140 yards (130m). A 90-yard (80-m) throw with return and a catch has been made. The highest number of consecutive catches is 129. One thrower once had ten boomerangs in flight at one time. The late Frank Donnellan of Australia was able to catch boomerangs blindfolded.

A good trick, which isn't too difficult, is to launch your boomerang slightly downwards so it hits the ground 5 or 10 yards (4·6 or 9·1m) in front of you. It will, if you are lucky, ricochet up, spinning wildly, and return (Fig. 31).

After some practice you should be able to perform several other tricks. Throw so that (a) the boomerang goes high, then slowly hovers down; (b) it passes you on the return, then comes back again; (c) it circles a post or tree and then returns.

Competitions are an ideal form of practice. See

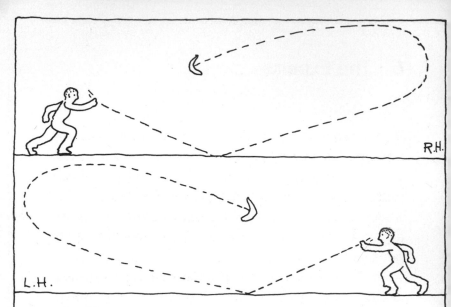

Fig. 31

who can throw a boomerang a certain distance (check with someone standing that distance away) and make it return the nearest. See who can keep a boomerang in flight for the longest time. My best time is 15 seconds. Let your friends throw their boomerangs, then throw yours to try and knock them out of the sky. Then, of course, let them try and hit yours. If you have two boomerangs, throw one and whilst it is in flight launch the next. When one lands, launch it again and see if you can keep one boomerang in flight all the time.

7 Other Boomerangs

High-speed, long-distance returning boomerangs are fun. These are as easy to make as the one I have described. To make a boomerang travel further and faster, simply make it heavier (use thicker plywood or perhaps fibreglass) and don't angle the tip so much or keep the tip flat. The sand paper grips mentioned in Chapter 4 are a great help in throwing. Throw it as hard as you can and spin it fast. Take a short run before you throw it, to give it more speed. You must never try to catch one of these high-speed boomerangs; they can be very dangerous.

Boomerangs can be other shapes. Some Aborigines used a boomerang in the shape of a cross. I have seen S-, Y- and X-shaped boomerangs. Some variations are shown in Fig. 6.

Indoor boomerangs about half the size of the wooden one I described can be constructed of balsa wood and will perform well in a large room or hall.

I hope you will have as much fun with your boomerangs as I have had with mine; one day we may be able to get boomerang throwing accepted as an Olympic sport.

One thing to remember about boomerangs is that if you get fed up with them, you won't be able to throw them away!

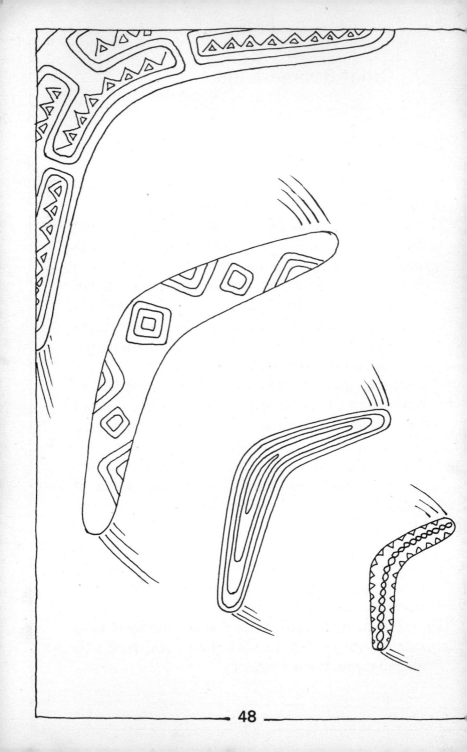